This book is a gift of
THE MORAGA
JUNIOR WOMEN'S
CLUB
Moraga Branch, Contra Costa County Library

Just Mommy and Me

This book is dedicated to my husband, Gino,
and my two beloved children,
Ilyse April and Ilijah A.
—T.J.M.

For my son, Eric,
who was my little monkey.
—K.B.

Just Mommy and Me

www.harperchildrens.com

Library of Congress Cataloging-in-Publication Data
Morrow, Tara Jaye.
Just Mommy and me / by Tara Jaye Morrow ; illustrated by Katy Bratun.
p. cm.
Summary: A monkey mother and child spend a wonderful day together, from morning bananas to sleeping under the moon.
ISBN 0-06-000724-9 ISBN 0-06-000725-7 (lib. bdg.)
[1. Mother and child—Fiction. 2. Monkeys—Fiction. 3. Stories in rhyme.] I. Bratun, Katy, ill. II. Title.
PZ8.3.C343 Ju 2004 2002001469
[E]—dc21 CIP
AC

Typography by Elynn Cohen 1 2 3 4 5 6 7 8 9 10 ❖
First Edition

Just Mommy and Me

by Tara Jaye Morrow • illustrated by Katy Bratun

HarperCollinsPublishers

If I were a monkey who swung on a tree

and you were my mommy, who swung after me,

and we ate bananas until there were none

and then took a nap in the warm, cozy sun

and when we woke up, sang our favorite song

while clapping and jumping and dancing along . . .

If we were two monkeys who played hide-and-seek
and I promised you, Mommy, that I wouldn't peek

and we took a walk in a cool, shady place

and saw who could make the silliest face

and we picked some flowers to put in your hat,
and I got to choose them—you know I'd love that!

If we were two monkeys just having a ball,

and we took a swim with the fishies and frogs
and splashed in the water and rolled on the logs

and snuggled up close while we looked at the skies

to watch the sun set and the stars wink their eyes . . .

If we did these things
all the day long, and soon,
we both fell asleep under
bright Mr. Moon . . .

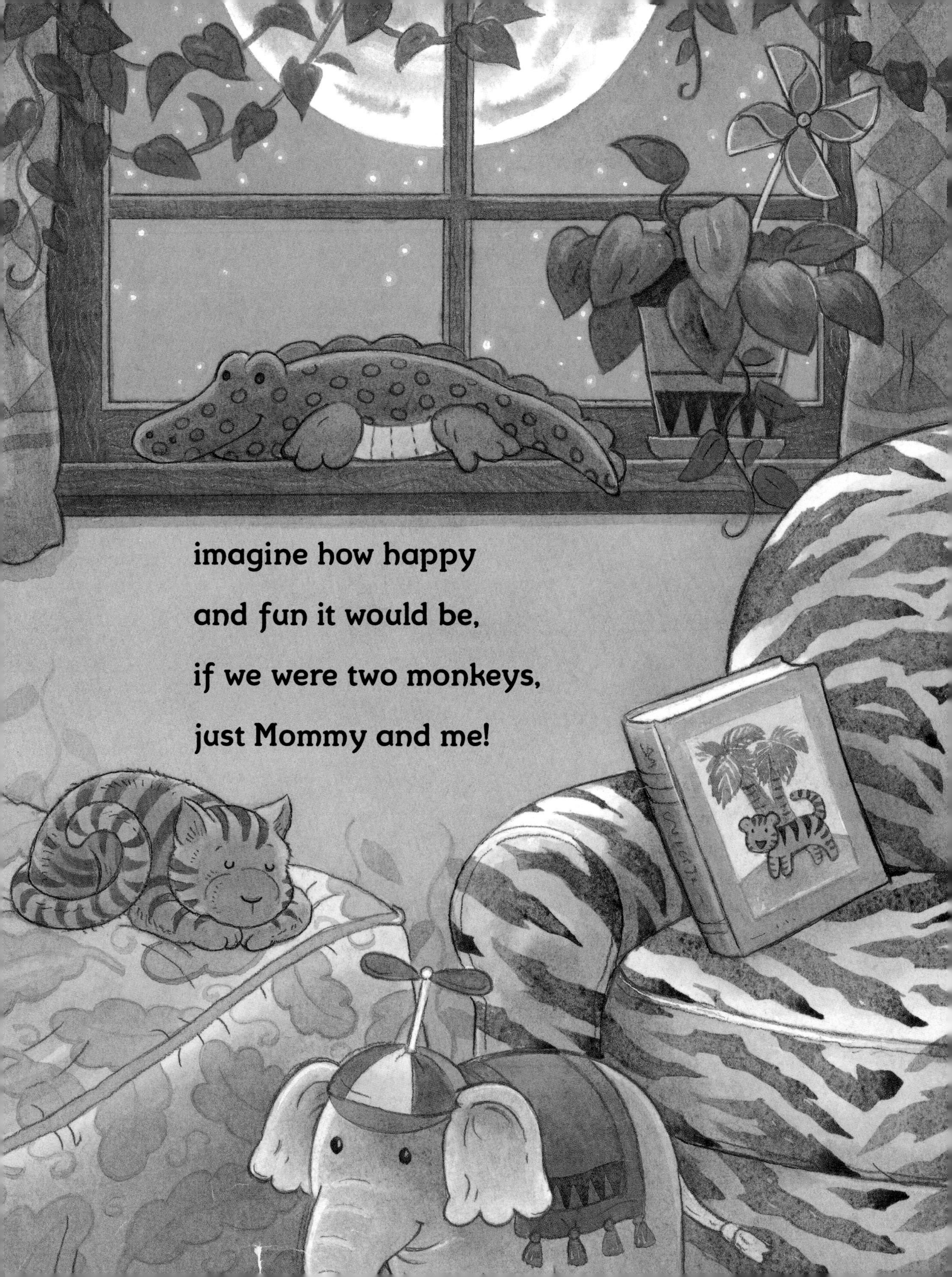

imagine how happy

and fun it would be,

if we were two monkeys,

just Mommy and me!